This edition published by Parragon Books Ltd in 2016 and distributed by

Parragon Inc.
440 Park Avenue South, 13th Floor
New York, NY 10016
www.parragon.com

Copyright © Parragon Books Ltd 2013-2016
Text © Hollins University

Written by Margaret Wise Brown
Illustrated by Charlotte Cooke

Edited by Michael Diggle
Designed by Kathryn Davies
Production by Jonathan Wakeham

ISBN 978-1-4748-6272-1

Printed in China

SUNSHINE
and
Snowballs

PaRragon

Bath • New York • Cologne • Melbourne • Delhi
Hong Kong • Shenzhen • Singapore

Summer, summer in the sun,

Flowers grow and bunnies run.

Snowballs, snowballs in the snow,

Snowflakes fall and cold winds blow.

Pussy willows in the spring,

Violets bloom and birds sing.

The wind blows hard across the hills,

And shakes the yellow daffodils.

Grasshoppers,
ladybugs,
and bees,

Hop

about,

bare toes and knees.

The fog comes on without a sound,

Gray, silent, all around.

Rain, rain on the windowpane,

Splashes once,

then splashes again.

Jagged lightning
splits the sky,

Thunder rumbles, wild winds cry!

Orange pumpkins, yellow corn,

Purple grapes and a frosty morn.

Smoke is drifting all around,

From raked leaves
on the ground.

Walk across the icy snow,

Footprints follow wherever you go.

Starlight, starlight, frosty bright,

Fills the spaces of the night.